Let your
take flight
Enjoy!
Susan Stafford

POCKET PEGASUS

POCKET PEGASUS

Flash and the Turtle Creek Triad

SUSAN STAFFORD

JESPERSON PUBLISHING

P.O. Box 2188, 100 Water Street, St. John's, NL, A1C 6E6
www.jespersonpublishing.ca

Library and Archives Canada Cataloguing in Publication

Stafford, Susan, 1954-

Pocket Pegasus : Flash and the Turtle Creek Triad / by Susan Stafford.

ISBN 978-1-894377-32-4

1. Horses–Juvenile fiction. I. Title.

PS8637.T325P62 2008 jC813'.6 C2008-905632-9

We acknowledge the financial support of The Canada Council for the Arts for our publishing activities.

We acknowledge the support of the Department of Tourism, Culture and Recreation for our publishing activities.

We acknowledge the financial support of the Government of Canada through the Book Publishing Industry Development Program (BPIDP) for our publishing activities.

Printed in Canada.

Acknowledgements

Special thanks to my test group of brave young book critics – Amanda, Alice, Josclyn, Emilee and Taylor.

Also, much appreciation to Karen Briggs, Nicole Kitchener and Catherine Scholz for their expert advice and words of encouragement.

Serious model horse collecters will know that the Breyer Mystical Pegasus mentioned in the story was never available for direct purchase, and as of this writing, is now retired. For the purposes of this tale, it was made available for sale.

Dedication

This book is dedicated to my children,
Dan, Laura and Ian, who provided
inspiration, to my mother, Alice, who waited
far too long, and to my husband, Ross,
who has always been my biggest fan.

Chapter 1

The summer had barely begun, but Laura Connor was already bored, bored, *bored.* With her thirteenth birthday still three weeks away, the petite blonde was considered too young to land a "real" summer job, such as working at a convenience store, gas bar or fast-food restaurant. She could easily have rounded up some babysitting clients in the small town of Turtle Creek where she lived, but to be honest, as an only child she really didn't like little kids that much.

What Laura really wanted to do was work at a stable. She had loved horses since she was old enough to point and squeal excitedly from her car seat at the "*Hossees!*" grazing in the fields outside of town. She read about them, wrote about them, drew pictures of them, daydreamed about owning one. It was not to be, however. Her parents, both musicians, could not risk such a long-term financial commitment. Their seven-piece party band, High Octane, was in huge demand during the busy summer season, but the high times were often followed by long, lean winters.

"It's feast or famine," Laura's mom, CeeCee, would say good-naturedly, but it was painfully close to the truth.

This was not to say that CeeCee and Tom Connor were irresponsible parents. There were lots of advantages to having a mom and dad who broke the nine-to-five mold. They were always around in the mornings to make Laura's lunch and drive her to school if the weather was nasty. They were often at home in the afternoons when she returned from school – unlike most of her friends, who came home to empty houses.

Weekend evenings, however, would find CeeCee and Tom off to a gig: a wedding, a dinner/dance, a black tie fundraiser. Until recently, Laura had been looked after on those occasions by an elderly neighbour, but her parents now felt their daughter was responsible enough to stay home alone. Laura enjoyed both the freedom and the solitude.

Their house was always full of music and laughter, especially when her parents' circle of friends, most of whom were also musicians, dropped in. Their summer barbeques were legendary. Her mom and dad were actually pretty cool, Laura thought – or at least as cool as parents could be.

Laura had long ago accepted that horse ownership was out of the question for her, but she did have one passion she could pursue: she collected model horses. Her collection numbered twenty-three so far, most received as birthday or Christmas gifts from her parents and relatives, and a few purchased with money she had earned delivering the weekly paper in Turtle Creek. Most of the models were Breyer or Stone creations: horses standing, running and jumping; quarter horses, arabians and thoroughbreds; foals, mares and stallions. Her bookcases were scattered with them, and she had even fashioned simple stalls out of shoeboxes and orange crates. All her models had names and birthdays.

Her very favourite model, however, was very different from the rest. He was made of porcelain, not plastic, and he was rearing, with forelegs raking the air, silver mane and tail flowing. He had wings, and he was *spectacular.*

Laura knew the statue was fashioned after Pegasus, the fabulous winged horse of mythology, but she thought that name was too stuffy, so she just called him Flash.

Flash did not reside in the bookcase with the rest of the herd. He was given a special place on the wide window seat in her room so that he could look outside at the world. Laura liked to believe that he enjoyed his position of privilege. She often rotated some of her other favourite models to the window bench to keep him company so he would not get lonely. He seemed to prefer the mares – or at least that was what she liked to think.

Laura's mother had found the unusual Pegasus figurine at an estate auction in Toronto when the family had vacationed there several years before. Laura had fallen in love with the statuette on the spot, and although the bidding went higher than her parents' agreed-upon spending limit, her mom determinedly raised her numbered paddle again and again until the gavel fell in their favour.

"Consider this your birthday *and* Christmas presents for the next three years," her dad had joked.

Laura turned away from her bedroom window, sighed and opened the local newspaper she had scooped from the kitchen table on her way upstairs. She spread the paper out on the bed and pored over the classified section, skipping over the ads for strange positions such as "boring mill operator" and "tool and die expert" (what was that, anyway?), looking for some kind of job with a title she actually understood.

Maxine, the family tabby, sprang onto the bed and plopped directly on the very section of paper Laura was reading.

"Beat it, Maxi," she said, annoyed.

Maxi purred loudly and stretched her considerable length and girth across the paper.

Laura eased the newspaper out from under the large cat and took it over to her window seat. She settled on a soft upholstered pillow and continued reading. Suddenly, she saw an item that tweaked her interest:

STABLE HELP WANTED:
Exp. pref. Part time incl. some wknds & heavy lifting. Call 519-555-3213.

Laura's eyes widened. Horses! She could do this. That is, as long as they overlooked the fact that she had little practical experience handling horses and was probably too small to sling heavy bags of grain around. Minor details.

Laura wondered which farm had placed the ad, as the number listed was a local one. She gathered up the newspaper and scampered downstairs. Maxi, startled, leaped off the bed and bolted down the steps as well, nearly taking Laura's legs out from under her.

"Mom? Mom!" Laura found her mother in the kitchen, frying bacon and making French toast. "I found a job I really, really want. It's on a farm. With horses and everything. Can I call about it?"

Mrs. Connor slid the French toast from frying

pan to plate. "*May* you call, you mean," she corrected. "Is it nearby? I don't mind driving you, as long as it's not three counties over."

"I'm pretty sure it is," Laura replied. "I'll call and find out right after breakfast." Laura added two strips of bacon to her plate and poured maple syrup over the fragrant, cinnamon-sprinkled eggy toast.

While she ate, she thought about what she would say when she answered the ad. *I have to sound really confident,* she thought. *I'll tell them I know a lot about horses, even if it is mostly from books and DVDs. What are my strong points? Well, I'm reliable, hard working...*

After tidying up the kitchen, Laura dialed the number. Four rings later, she was listening to a woman who bore the slightest hint of an English accent: "Good morning. Banbury Cross Stables."

Laura swallowed hard and dove right in. "My name is Laura Connor and I'm calling about your ad in the paper for part-time stable help."

"Oh, lovely," the woman replied. "Our regular girl broke her leg in a riding accident, and most young people already have their summer jobs lined up, so we're very keen to hire someone straight away. Do you have much experience? How old are you, dear?"

"I'm, uh, thirteen." Laura winced and corrected herself. "Next month, actually. I really, really love horses, and all animals, and I mucked out stalls once with my friend Krissy at her uncle's farm in Blackstock. They have Belgians and one of them stepped on my foot and I'm really reliable and I'll work so hard, you won't regret hiring me, I promise..." Her voice tailed off. *Yikes,* she thought, *I'm babbling like a crazy person.*

Banbury Cross lady laughed. "Well, you're certainly enthusiastic! We really were looking for someone a bit older, but I suppose you could come out to the farm and we'll have a chat, at least. My name is Mrs. Leeds, by the way."

Mrs. Leeds gave Laura directions, which she relayed to her mother. They agreed to meet at two o'clock that afternoon.

Laura hung up the phone and bounced like a cheerleader across the kitchen. "I can't wait! This is so awesome! Oh!" She had a thought. "I have to do some research." With that, she bounded upstairs. She powered up the computer in the den and spent the next hour and a half on her favourite horse-related internet sites, absorbing information on equine nutrition, stable skills and horse management.

When she finished, she knew by heart that a 1,000-pound horse in light work requires 15 to 20 pounds of hay each day, that oats come in crimped, rolled or whole form, that you always lead a horse from the left, that the feed-room door should always be locked. Horses are groomed from the top down using brushes that progress from coarse to fine. They need up to 12 gallons of clean water every day, even in the winter.

"And their hooves need trimming every six to eight weeks," Laura announced with satisfaction to no one in particular.

Feeling much better prepared for the interview, Laura stretched, reached over to turn the computer off, then hesitated. She signed onto her email account and fired off a message to her best friend, Krissy Martineau.

> Hey K, got a job interview this afternoon. At a real horse farm. Sounds sweet.
> L8R,
> L.

Chapter 2

The day seemed to creep along at a painfully slow pace. Laura passed the time by helping weed the front yard flowerbeds with her mom, and tidying her room. She showered and changed into a nice pair of working jeans, a t-shirt and paddock boots. Laura pulled her hair up into a ponytail, secured it with a scrunchy, and took a final glance in the mirror.

The bright June day was already becoming quite hazy and humid, and thunderstorms were forecast for the evening. Laura gazed out the window at the distant billowing thunderheads as the minivan headed north through town.

"I wonder how much the job pays?" she said.

"Make sure that's not your first question," cautioned Mrs. Connor. "I'm sure the farm owner will want your biggest concern to be the welfare of the horses."

"I know, and it is," Laura replied. "I'd probably do it for free, just to be able to hang around the barn."

"Well, let's not get too carried away," said her mother, laughing.

Turtle Creek was a pretty little community with a river winding through the centre of the grandly named "business district," which consisted only of a couple of clothing stores, a bakery, a gas station, a bank and a church.

"Clean and safe," her parents said proudly of their town.

"Lame," Laura complained to her friends.

There wasn't much for kids to do in The Creek – no bowling alley, no theatre, no skateboard park. Adults loved it, though, for the wine festivals hosted by local vineyards, street parties, concerts by the river, and art exhibits in the park. For Laura, the real fun took place thirty kilometres north in the "big city," where the family occasionally ventured to shop at the mall or take in a movie.

Between the small town and the bright city lights lay thousands of acres of farm land. Most were occupied by corn and soybean crops, but there were also, to Laura's delight, horse farms of every description. Thoroughbred and standardbred breeding operations churned out the winners and losers at several local racetracks. The riding stables had fields dotted with sturdy school ponies, while the boarding barns sported paddocks enclosing leggy dressage horses and hunters and jumpers. And then there were the private farms, with a couple of fat family horses grazing in the front yard.

Fifteen minutes later, the van pulled into a long, maple-lined driveway. Banbury Cross Stables was one of the tidiest farms Laura had ever seen. The barn and outbuildings were freshly painted, and the old cobblestone house was surrounded by neat lawns and gardens.

"Wow, this is nice," Laura said in awe. "Mrs. Leeds said to meet her in the barn."

They parked and walked through the stable's airy aisles. A fit, fiftyish woman standing outside the office greeted them warmly. "You must be Laura," she said, smiling and extending her hand. "Welcome to Banbury Cross Stables." She repeated the gesture with Mrs. Connor.

"It's so beautiful here," Laura gushed. "You're so lucky!"

"Come on, I'll give you the tour." Mrs. Leeds walked them through the barn. "This facility is set up for a dozen horses, but we currently only have six in residence. Two belong to boarders, and the other four are ours. We like to keep a mare in foal, and have a buy/sell horse as well."

They walked down the spacious aisle that smelled of fresh, fragrant wood shavings and something faintly medicinal. Liniment? Antiseptic? Through the far door were four large paddocks. Three horses occupied the nearest.

"This is Phantom, Dudley and Smidge," Mrs. Leeds said, indicating a lanky grey gelding, a large bay warmblood and a very small black pony. The trio raised their heads from grazing in the lush, early summer grass to stare inquisitively at the intruding humans.

"Over here we have Morning Glory, Bates Motel, whose stable name is Psycho, and Alba de Oro. Alba – her name means golden dawn in Spanish, apparently – is in foal to Bikini Bay, a really nice thoroughbred sire whose babies have done well at the track."

The dark bay mare stared aloofly at Laura from across the paddock, but Glory and Psycho, the two chestnuts, sauntered over to investigate Laura's outstretched hand. She laughed as she patted the gelding nicknamed Psycho. "He seems sane enough."

"On the ground, he's a sweetie," Mrs. Leeds admitted, "but put someone on his back and it's a different story."

They re-entered the barn, and Mrs. Leeds took Laura and her mother through the organized tack room, feed room and finally, the office, where they were invited to sit.

"So, Laura." Mrs. Leeds came straight to the point. "What makes you so sure you're the one for the job?"

For the next few minutes, Laura explained her lifelong addiction to horses, her vast (albeit book-learned) knowledge, and limited hands-on experience. She provided the names and phone numbers of some character references: a favourite teacher, the supervisor at the local newspaper, and her friend's uncle.

Mrs. Leeds looked thoughtfully at the young girl for several moments, then rose from behind her desk. "How does this sound? Because you are the first person to answer the ad, I'd like to give it a week in case there are any other interested people who would like to apply. I do like you. I think you're smart and eager and will try hard. You could learn a lot with supervision, which I would be happy to provide. I promise I will give you fair consideration, in spite of your age, when I make my decision."

Laura's shoulders sagged; this was not what she wanted to hear. A week? That seemed like a very long time to wait. But she smiled anyway, shook Mrs. Leeds' hand and said, "Thanks, I appreciate that."

"We'll be looking forward to your call," said Mrs. Connor. She put her arm around Laura's slim shoulders and gently steered her toward the door.

The day was becoming increasingly gloomy and oppressive, which was reflected in Laura's mood. They drove home in relative silence; none of Laura's bubbly optimism remained.

"Well, I thought that went pretty well," Mrs. Connor finally offered. "I'm proud of you."

Laura shrugged. "I'm afraid that someone older and better will come along in the next week, and I won't get the job."

While her mother didn't disagree, she tried to sound positive. "Keep your fingers crossed. On a different subject, remember that your dad and I have a job tonight. It's from eight to midnight, so we probably won't get home much before one or one-thirty."

"I'll be fine, Mom. There's a good movie on tonight and I'm gonna make a huge bowl of popcorn and snuggle with Maxi."

By seven o'clock, her parents were packed up and ready to head out to work. Laura waved goodbye at the front steps as they pulled out of the driveway. She closed the door firmly and locked it, then headed upstairs to email Krissy again with the less-than-awesome news about the stable job.

It was very hot. Laura threw open a window and more sultry, humid air wafted in, driven by a slight breeze. She logged onto MSN to see if Krissy was online…yes! The next hour flew by as the pair chatted about everything and nothing.

Laura and Krissy had been close friends since grade two when Laura was the new kid at school and Krissy had taken pity on her. They had embarked on many adventures together, gotten into trouble a time or two, swapped clothes, shared a case of chicken pox and more than a couple of flu viruses. Krissy's birthday was only three days after Laura's, and they liked to pretend they were sisters.

With a bit of time to kill before her movie started, Laura puttered in her room, dusting and rearranging her models and deciding which mare would occupy the place of honour beside Flash in the window. She chose a Lipizzaner performing the distinctive Spanish walk, neck arched and right foreleg stepping boldly ahead. She thought they made a handsome couple.

Running her index finger along the top of the row of books in the bookcase, Laura pulled out one of her mythology and legends volumes and flipped to the section on Pegasus. She knew the story by heart, but always enjoyed reading about fantasy and myths, dragons, unicorns, and other fabulous creatures.

As the story went, Pegasus was the magnificent winged horse that was the offspring of the Gorgon Medusa and Poseidon, ruler of the sea. When the Greek hero, Perseus, cut off Medusa's head of snakes, Pegasus was born. The goddess Athena was the first to catch Pegasus. She presented another warrior, Bellerophon, with a golden bridle with which he was able to ride Pegasus. Together, the pair slew the monster Chimera, but when Bellerophon attempted to ride Pegasus to Mount Olympus to visit the gods, he was thrown off. The job of Pegasus from that point on was to bring thunderbolts to Zeus. His name, in fact, is thought to have come from the Luwian word for lightning, *pihassas.* It was said that wherever Pegasus' hoof struck the earth, a spring would burst forth.

According to some stories, Pegasus took a wife later in life, and the pair began a family which became the origin of all winged horses. When he died, Pegasus rose to the heavens, where he became a constellation of stars.

Several hours later, movie viewed and popcorn eaten, Laura decided to turn in. Upstairs, with the windows open and the curtains wafting gently in the breeze, she heard thunder rumbling in the distance. This did not bother her much. While she used to be terrified of storms, her dad had patiently sat with her on the window bench, storm after storm, pointing out the different types and colours of the lightning, teaching her to count between the flash and the thunder to estimate the distance of the strike. She learned to appreciate the pinkish cloud-to-cloud illumination of summer heat lightning, and had once even smelled the pungent ozone smell seared into the air following a particularly close strike.

Not a scared little kid anymore, now Laura would simply listen to her little MP3 player if the racket from a storm kept her awake. This particular squall was approaching very fast. She popped in her earbuds, pulled a light sheet over her and closed her eyes.

Maxine, who had been curled up among the throw pillows on the window seat, stood, yawned and did her best Hallowe'en cat stretch. Lightning dramatically backlit the feline's form. Laura saw this apparition through half-closed eyes and smiled. It would have almost been creepy, except for the fact that Maxi was kind of overweight – well, *really* overweight – which ruined the whole effect. Laura giggled and closed her eyes.

The fat cat, moving to take her place on the quilt at the foot of Laura's bed, jumped less than gracefully to the floor. The effort sent a pillow skidding backward into Flash and his girlfriend-*du-jour.* The Lipizzaner teetered and then settled back onto her dainty hooves. Flash tipped to the side, leaning precariously against the window frame like a tiny drunken fairy.

The storm raged outside. Trees in the town square were whipped by the wind, and flashes of lightning illuminated the pelting rain.

In one simultaneous, thunderous moment, lightning hit the rooster weather vane atop the Connors' house. The huge surge of power swept across the rain-soaked roof, along the eaves and into the metal trim of the upstairs windows. Three hundred thousand volts entered the little porcelain Pegasus at the point where his head and chest rested against the frame. A hot silver glow spread across his body to the tips of his wings, then slowly faded.

Laura woke with a yelp. She tossed the earbuds aside, heart pounding, and sat up, terrified. She could smell something strange, something hot and disturbingly foreign. Was something on fire? Had lightning hit a tree outside? Had lightning hit the house?

She snapped out of her stupor and turned on her bedside lamp. Good, the power wasn't out. But what was that odd smell?

Downstairs, Laura found the answer. The cord to the old television set in the spare room was blackened and melted. She gingerly pulled the plug from the wall socket and dropped it to the floor. It was very hot. She ran her hand down the wall near the socket, but it seemed cool enough. She was pretty sure there were no flames smouldering inside. The same seemed true of the TV – now ex-TV.

Satisfied that the house was in no immediate danger of going up in flames, the shaken girl continued her inspection.

In the kitchen, it appeared that the microwave had suffered the same fate as the TV. Laura carefully unplugged the sticky black wire and laid it on the counter. Room by room, with Maxi trailing curiously behind her and complaining loudly, she checked all the appliances and found no more casualties. She glanced at the clock; her parents would be home in about an hour and a half. She decided to stay awake until they returned. She doubted she could get back to sleep anyway.

Laura scooped up Maxi and carried her upstairs, then stopped abruptly. The computer! She hoped it had been spared from incineration. As she pushed the power button, she remembered with relief that they had wisely installed a surge protector just a couple of months earlier. She typed a quick message to Krissy, which made her feel a bit less alone, more connected to the outside world.

```
Hey K:
House was just hit by lightning
(I think). Fried one of our TVs
and the microwave was nuked.
Scared the poop out of me!
T@YL.
L.
```

As quickly as it had arrived, the storm moved off to terrorize some other community with its wrath. Back in bed, her jittery nerves calmed considerably, Laura fought to keep her eyes focused on the horsey teen novel she was reading. Slowly, slowly, her sleepy lids closed.

Chapter 3

"*Nichew!*"

Laura's eyes fluttered open. She lay motionless, heart pounding, still lying on her back with the open book on her chest. She listened…listened…

"*Nicheeeew!*"

It was a sneeze. A very tiny sneeze, like a mouse with allergies. She sat bolt upright. Maxi was still on the bed, but the feline's gaze was focused intently on something by the window. Laura squinted. Something was missing. Flash! The white mare was still in her place on the window seat, but Flash was gone.

Thinking the winged figurine had fallen off onto the floor – and shattered? She hoped not – Laura eased out of bed and tiptoed over to the window, careful not to step on any broken bits in her bare feet. The floor, however, was bare – no tiny ears or hooves or amputated wingtips. So where was he?

Suddenly, one of the throw cushions moved. Once, then twice, it wobbled. Again, Laura was paralyzed with fear. To her horror, an elegant white nose appeared, followed by a slender alabaster feathered wing, which sprouted from between the brocade fabrics. The pillows parted and Flash stood to his full height and slowly flapped his magnificent wings.

He spoke. "Hello, Laura."

Laura shrieked and fell backward, running into the bedpost, hard, in her panic and haste to get to the doorway.

"Oh, please don't be frightened," said the voice. "I'm so sorry I woke you, but it was all the cat hair in the cushions, you see... I've been needing to sneeze for years."

The voice, Flash's voice, was pleasant and actually rather soothing, and a bit cultured. *Like Niles Crane on those old* Frasier *reruns,* was the odd comparison Laura's racing mind spat out. She found her heart rate slowing somewhat as she watched from the doorway, absently rubbing the painful spot on her thigh that was surely going to bruise in a most spectacular way.

Why hadn't she run downstairs and phoned for help? Laura wondered. *But who ya gonna call,* her brain taunted. *Ghostbusters? The police? 9-1-1?* She could just imagine how well *that* conversation would go...

> *Hello, this is the 9-1-1 operator. What is the nature of your emergency?*
>
> *Well, there's an eight-inch flying horse – talking flying horse – standing in my bedroom.*
>
> *Hmmm, I see... Perhaps you would be better off calling Animal Control, dear... Click.*

Laura inched forward to get a better look at the little feathered marvel. Flash – if that was really his name – reared up to his full height and flapped his wings luxuriously. He landed and snaked his neck one way, and then the other. Laura detected the tiniest pop as he cracked out his spine.

"Ahhh, that feels much better. Now, I'm ready for some fun," he said brightly.

Cautiously, Laura perched on the edge of her bed. "Who are you? How did this happen? Where did you..."

Flash launched himself off the window seat, flapped lazily across the room and landed gently on the bed beside Laura. "Well, I'm not exactly sure. The last thing I remember was being sent into battle against the evil wizard Malvenom during the War of Elysia. That was a long, long time ago – centuries, I suspect." He cast a glance over his shoulder at his diminutive frame. "It appears I lost the fight."

Laura slowly put out her hand. "May I... May I touch you?" she asked shyly.

"Of course!" came the immediate and enthusiastic reply. "In fact, I have a terrible itch behind my left wing. Could you?" Flash extended the wing in question and looked beseechingly at her. His eyes! They were piercing and golden, like those of an eagle.

A little shakily, Laura touched his silvery coat,

trailing her fingers along his back and dipping behind his near-side wing to gently scratch the offending itch.

"Aaaaaah," Flash sighed appreciatively.

Laura's hand strayed along the length of his wing. The feeling was hypnotizing, tantalizing. The sensation of muscle and feathers, strength and softness, was both strange and sensual.

A light suddenly reflected off the window panes. Laura gasped. "It's my parents! What am I going to tell them? Quick, you'd better hide."

"But why?" Flash protested.

"Just do it. Please!" Laura begged. "I haven't had time to figure out what to tell them about you – if I tell them." The little winged equine scampered across the rumpled bed and wriggled under a pillow. Laura turned off the light and raced down the stairs to greet her parents.

CeeCee, elegant in her black evening dress, and Tom, tall and handsome in his tuxedo, were surprised to see Laura still up at this hour. They listened intently to her tale of thunderstorms and smoking appliances. She did leave a *few* details out. There was no mention, for instance, of Flash's reincarnation.

Laura was still not sure how to broach the subject without sounding completely insane. She was beginning to feel rather protective of the little horse, and although she had never kept secrets from her parents before, this situation seemed somehow different.

After giving her parents a quick kiss goodnight, Laura started to head back to her room, then changed her mind and detoured to the kitchen. She poked through the pantry, finally deciding on a handful of Cheerios, which she placed in a small plastic container and smuggled upstairs.

"Flash? Flash?" she whispered as she closed her bedroom door. His elegant little head arose from the pile of pillows leaning against the headboard.

"I brought you something to eat. I figured you might be hungry after all this time. I hope you like it. It's the only thing I could think of in a pinch." She placed the container on the bed.

Flash bounded from his hiding place with unbridled glee. "I really am rather peckish. I haven't eaten in, well, eons!" He sniffed the oaty little rings, bit a piece off one and chewed thoughtfully. "Oh, these are quite tasty!" he exclaimed, and tucked into the pile enthusiastically.

When there was nothing left but crumbs, Laura padded quietly down the hall to the bathroom, where she rinsed out the container and filled it with cool, fresh water.

Flash drank long and deeply. "That was lovely, thank you," he said politely, wiping his muzzle on his foreleg when he was done.

He circled a couple of times on the bed. *Like a dog making a nest,* Laura thought. Then he collapsed with a little *whoomph* and smoothed his wings back against his silky flanks.

"I have so many questions," Laura began.

"Ask away," Flash invited. "But I may not have the answers to all of them."

For the next half hour, Laura and Flash quietly conversed in the dark bedroom. From what Flash could recollect, he had been encased in the porcelain figurine for several centuries, as the result of having been on the losing end of a battle with the evil wizard Malvenom. The powerful spell had frozen him in mid-attack: forelegs pawing the air, wings fully outstretched, neck arched, mane and tail flowing.

"I remember him pointing a long, bony finger at me, then a bright flash, but the details of exactly how I ended up here are a little fuzzy. It seems my first owner found me in some British woods, the Devil's Elbow Forest, I believe, while he was out hunting. He was a very wealthy, decent English gentleman, and I adorned his mantle until his death. I was sold at auction with the rest of his estate to an oddities dealer, then had several more homes via a few antique stores both in Europe and eventually here in North America. Some of my owners were nice, and some were rather eccentric. Then your mother purchased me. I was a steal, you know."

Flash snickered a horsey nicker snicker. "No one could ever guess my worth, as I had no identifying marks or artist's signature, or even a date. To be quite honest, I was a bit worried when I saw that my new keeper was just a child – no offense. I thought it was the end of the road for me, that I would be smashed to pieces by accident, but your care has been exemplary."

Laura wasn't sure what *exemplary* meant, but it sounded like a good thing, and she was pleased.

"I resided quite happily in your window, until tonight, when there was a huge flash of light and a positively electrifying sensation."

Of course, Laura thought. *The bolt of lightning that hit the house must have gone through him and somehow reversed the spell.*

"I think it was the lightning," Laura said. "It's been known to do some really strange things. Did you know that your chances of being struck are about one in three million?"

While Flash was mulling that figure over, Laura suddenly yawned. Much to her surprise, she found she was quite exhausted. "I have to get some sleep now, Flash. Do you mind if I call you Flash?"

"Not at all, Mistress Laura," he insisted. "But I've been asleep for centuries. I want to do something."

"Tomorrow. I promise we'll have fun tomorrow. And just call me Laura. But now, sleep."

Flash settled in between the two pillows at the head of the bed. Moments later, his gentle snoring filled the air.

Chapter 4

Laura awoke to a morning chorus of birds chattering in the trees outside her windows. For a moment, the events of the night before seemed like a distant dream, then her head rolled to the left and she realized that the impossible was in fact very real. And it was sitting on its haunches, looking at her.

"Good morning," Flash greeted her, bright-eyed.

Laura desperately needed a plan. What was she going to do with her little flying companion? Should she tell her parents? Should she tell anybody?

She hurriedly made her bed while Flash flapped

lazily around the room, exploring. He settled on the bookshelf with the rest of the models, tipping over the end one and causing the rest to topple like a row of dominoes. "So sorry," he apologized, head hanging.

As Laura moved to set the models upright, there was a soft knock on her door.

"Hey, what's going on in there?"

Laura froze. It was her mother. She looked at Flash in panic as the door handle turned.

"Good morning, honey. What's all the racket?"

Laura turned to face her mother. "I, uh, just knocked over some of my models by accident."

Looking back at her bookcase, she was grateful to see Flash, frozen motionless in his familiar rearing pose, looking very statue-like. He winked at Laura. Hiding a smile, Laura continued to hurriedly straighten the models, then ushered her mom out the door.

"I'm starved. What's for breakfast?"

With a full tummy and a pocketful of Cheerios,

Laura trotted upstairs to see if Flash was hungry. He was pacing unhappily in the window.

"What's wrong?" Laura asked, concerned.

"I, um, would really like to go outside. Actually, I really need to go outside, if you catch my meaning."

Laura was about to argue that such a thing was impossible when she realized that he needed to answer "the call of nature," as her dad always referred to it.

"Just a sec," she said, pulling on sweats and a hoodie over her pjs. She glanced around her room for a suitable conveyance for her little refugee. Her gaze settled on her pink school backpack, now empty of books and pens. She shook it upside down to dump out the last of the crumpled bits of paper. "Quick, get in here."

Flash looked doubtfully into the open bag, then gingerly stepped inside. Laura carefully zipped the bag up, hung it over one shoulder and went downstairs to the kitchen. "I'm going out for a bit, Mom," Laura announced. "To the park, and to see if Krissy's home."

The street on which she lived dead-ended at a small parkette. It was empty, much to Laura's relief. She knelt down in a secluded grassy section surrounded by a tall hedge and released Flash from his stuffy prison. He burst out of the bag and rose in a spiral, obviously delighted to feel the sun on his wings again. After a quick and discreet trip to the bushes, he galloped happily back to Laura. He scampered around her like a little pixie, nibbled at some lush grass, and then looked speculatively upwards. "What's next?"

Laura had been trying to figure out her next move. This news was too big to keep bottled up. She felt as though she would burst. She needed to spill the beans to *somebody*.

"Come on, Flash, back in the bag."

He looked crestfallen.

"It won't be for long, I promise."

Stashed away and zipped up, Flash was transported a couple of blocks away to the little sidesplit where Krissy lived. Laura had to knock several times before her disheveled friend answered the door, still in her pajamas.

"'Sup?" she mumbled sleepily, idly scratching her backside.

"Let me in. I have something to show you,"

Laura said, holding up the backpack.

"What is it? Did you get a new model?" Krissy slowly came to life. "I know, it's a real pony," she joked. "Or maybe a miniature horse."

"Way better than that," Laura said. "Where are your mom and dad?"

Krissy scanned the driveway. "Out shopping, I guess. The car is gone."

Laura pushed past her into the kitchen. Krissy trotted along behind, cobwebs gone and curiosity level high. Carefully, Laura tipped the opened backpack forward and Flash slid gracefully onto the counter.

There was a long silence. Krissy finally spoke. "Wow," she breathed.

"He was trapped in that figurine of mine for centuries by an evil wizard, then lightning hit him last night during the storm." Laura continued relaying the tale, words tumbling over each other, finishing breathlessly, "Isn't he awesome?"

Flash clip-clopped across the counter to stand in front of Krissy. "So nice to meet you," he said, bowing slightly.

Krissy's jaw dropped. "He *talks*, too? Ohmigod."

The girls chattered excitedly while Flash explored the kitchen. So many new wonders caught his attention: the cookie jar shaped like a frog, the tall jars of colourful peppers in olive oil. He hovered in front of the shiny, stainless steel fridge, admiring his own reflection, and was fascinated when Krissy showed him how the icemaker worked.

"I have to go back home and do chores," Laura finally said. "My mom and dad are working again tonight. Do you want to sleep over?"

Krissy thought that was a most excellent idea and promised to ask her parents' permission the minute they got home.

Heading back home with Flash safely, although reluctantly, tucked into the backpack, Laura tried to plan her day so that she would not be far from the little guy. Going to the mall was out – too many people, not to mention the long car trip. She would offer to weed the vegetable garden, she decided, which would surely cause raised eyebrows from her parents. At least Flash wouldn't have to stay cooped up inside on such a nice day. He would have to promise to mind her, though, so as not to be spotted by the neighbours.

Laura's parents were both surprised and delighted by her sudden interest in yardwork. Before heading to the hardware store to pick up material for a long-overdue garden shed and a new microwave to replace the old incinerated one, they made sure Laura was outfitted with a hat, gloves, sunscreen and a trowel.

Alone in the quiet corner garden, Laura once again freed the impatient Flash, but not before she "read him the riot act," as her mom loved to say. "You have to stay out of sight below the fenceline, or else the neighbours or people walking by on the sidewalk might see you, which would be a very bad thing. And if I say get back in the bag *now*, I mean it."

Flash sighed and scraped a tiny hoof in the dirt. "But why can't people be allowed to see me? I don't want to be in hiding forever."

Why indeed? Laura had thought long and hard about this. She patiently explained that if the whole world knew about the little flying horse, he would likely be taken from her to be studied by scientists, or put on display in some zoo, or hounded by the press and paparazzi, or have people wanting him as some sort of exotic pet. She shuddered at the thought. Flash – this living, breathing version of Flash – had been in her life barely twelve hours and already she could not bear the thought of ever being separated from him.

Weeding turned out to be far more fun than Laura expected. Flash watched quietly at first, until he figured out what the basic idea of weeding entailed. Then he wholeheartedly pitched in, ripping out the smaller green intruders with his teeth and digging out the dandelions and thistles with his sharp front hooves. Dirt and weeds flew, and the pair were finished in record time, the rows neatly raked, the weeds heaped in the compost pile. As a reward, Flash received a tiny, tender baby carrot, which he ate with slobbery gusto.

The two of them were in the living room watching *Animal Planet.* Flash was amazed by the "television machine," and quickly decided that this was his favourite channel. A noise outside indicated that Laura's parents had returned, the creaky old family pickup filled with lumber and boxes.

"Quick, get upstairs," Laura hissed, releasing Flash into the air like a dove. He swooped up the stairway and out of sight.

"Could you help us unload the truck, honey?" CeeCee called from the doorway. "We have to play a wedding at five o'clock and we're running a little late."

Hauling the two-by-fours from the tailgate to the backyard turned out to be quite a workout for Laura's arms and back muscles.

"This will help you get in shape for working at the farm," her mom noted. "Make you all buff and stuff."

The job! Laura had completely forgotten about Banbury Cross and Mrs. Leeds. "Yeah, right," Laura giggled. "I'll be strong like bull, smart like toaster."

Her mother dropped a heavy armload of lumber onto the pile, where it rattled noisily and slid onto the grass.

"By the way, have you decided what you might like to do on your birthday? It's only a couple of weeks away, in case you've forgotton." She winked. "Thirteen years old, holy cow." Laura's mother launched into her nostalgic "it-seems-like-just-yesterday, where-have-the-years-gone?" speech she revived every year about this time.

Laura threw her arms around her mom's neck. "Oh, Mom, you're still as young and beautiful as the day I was born. And no, I'm still not sure what I want to do. Maybe see a movie? Or dinner at Outback? Or maybe Chinese?"

Krissy arrived breathlessly just as Laura's parents, toting instruments and gear – CeeCee with a silver gown and Tom with a white tuxedo slung over their shoulders – were packing up to leave. Once the van had rounded the corner out of sight, Krissy burst out, "So, where is he!?"

The girls bounded upstairs, armed with chips and Cheerios, and found Flash exploring long-forgotten items in Laura's cluttered closet with great interest. He had pulled out some sparkly Barbie clothes, a Baby Furby and a well-worn My Little Pony. BeDazzle beads and sequins littered the floor.

"Flash, you're making a mess," Laura cried, not

really upset at all. "Get out of there. We brought you a snack."

As they munched, Krissy asked her own set of questions. Flash patiently repeated his story, at least those parts he could remember.

"Were there others like you, or were you the only, you know, Pegasus?" Krissy wanted to know.

"Oh my, there were thousands of us," Flash began. "We lived peacefully in the forests and fields of Elysia, until the warring Troglodynes began to migrate southward, slaughtering and feasting on everything in their path. We could not flee into the mountains; there was not enough forage or food to sustain our families. So we had no choice but to stay and fight.

"Luckily, we were able to form an alliance with the neighbouring Valkyrians, who also did not want to be overrun by the Troglodynes. They were fierce fighters, descended from a race of dragon-riders, and we suited each other well. The Troglodynes, sensing that our combined defenses were too powerful to overcome, sought help from the Odious Brotherhood of Wizards, a branch of sorcerers that had been banished from the Free World many years before because of the dark magic they practiced."

Flash paused, the memory still painful. "The next time we met, our forces were decimated. It was a brutal, bloody battle, and when I found myself face-to-face with Malvenom himself, I was unable to avoid his evil magic. That's the last thing I remember before becoming aware that I was, well, trapped in a statue."

"That's awful," Laura said sadly. She envisioned the horrific battle, all the beautiful winged horses and brave warriors who fought to their deaths. "What about the others? What about your family?"

Flash looked down and idly scuffed a hoof on the carpet. "I don't know. My brother fought hard by my side. I am hoping that my sire and dam and little sister made it safely into the mountains. Even though it would have been a struggle to survive the harsh conditions there, at least they would have had a chance to live."

The trio sat in silence for a bit. Laura wished she could say something clever or soothing or inspirational, but nothing came.

Maxi entered the room, yawning. Her attention was suddenly riveted on the girls, and especially on their little companion. To feline eyes, Flash looked like lunch.

When the girls rose and headed for the office, Maxi saw her chance. Laura and Krissy had barely sat down in front of the computer when they heard a crash and a squeal. They rushed back into the bedroom. Maxi was running across the floor, dragging Flash by one wing like a lion wrestling an eagle. His free wing beat furiously against her face, and his sharp hooves flailed against her chest.

Before Laura could reach the struggling pair, Flash landed a particularly well-aimed blow and the cat released her grip long enough to allow his escape.

"Maxi!" Laura shrieked. "Bad cat!"

Maxi crouched, growling sullenly.

A thorough examination of the little horse revealed nothing broken or bleeding, although a pinfeather was badly crumpled. Flash roused his wings irritably and Laura realized that he was both annoyed and embarrassed. His golden eyes flashed, but did not meet hers.

"It's okay, Flash," Laura said, fighting back a smile.

"No, it's not!" he shot back. "I used to be a stealthy and fearless warrior. I fought monsters and all manner of vile creatures, and then that...that *thing* sneaks up on me as if I were a rank amateur." His voice, and apparently his displeasure, faded. He shot an evil glance at the cat, who had moved on to cleaning her paws with steady strokes of her pink tongue.

Laura scooped up the unhappy little warrior and suggested they all watch TV. "I'll let you have the remote," she promised.

Flash brightened, the incident forgotten.

The next few days passed in a busy, happy blur. Laura and Flash fell into a comfortable routine of meals and chores and fun. She became very adept at moving the little stowaway from room to room to garden to park to Krissy's house without being spotted. Laura even broke down and took Flash to the mall in the city, transporting him by backpack. He was entranced by the stores and shoppers, peeking discreetly from the backpack's zippered pouch. Laura bought him a dollar-store rhinestone bracelet which he wore proudly around his neck. She thought it was kind of girlie, but he seemed to love shiny things so much that she didn't want to spoil the moment.

Flash especially liked the pet store and was charmed by the cockatoos, who exceeded him in size and wingspan. One large sulfur-crested male caught sight of him and squawked loudly, his bright feathered crest rising to full plume like a crazy mohawk. Laura had to leave the store when all the birds took up the agitated cry and hopped from perch to perch, flapping and cheeping in excitement. The sales clerks glared at her accusingly as she rushed out the door.

On Thursday morning, the phone rang. It was Mrs. Leeds at Banbury Cross Stables. Mrs. Connor held her hand over the receiver and asked Laura, "You're still interested in the job, aren't you?" She had been puzzled by her daughter's distracted attitude in the past week. She had hardly even mentioned the barn.

"Of course I'm still interested," Laura insisted, grabbing the phone. "Hello?" She tried not to sound too eager or desperate, nor too indifferent.

"Well, Miss Connor, of all the people I have interviewed, I still like you the best. The job is yours if you still want it."

Laura's resolve broke. "Yes!" she squealed. "That's awesome. I mean, thank you, Mrs. Leeds. You won't be disappointed, I promise."

Mrs. Leeds told her to report to the farm at seven o'clock the following morning. Her mom assured Laura that providing a ride at that early hour was not a problem during the week, but they agreed that Laura would ride her bike if she was called in on the weekends, to allow her parents to sleep in after working a late night.

Laura hurried upstairs to share the exciting news with Flash. He did not seem to grasp the concept of horse-keeping on a large scale.

"They don't run free? They're kept in little cages indoors? Who feeds them? You mean humans actually fancy that they *own* creatures such as these?" He was aghast.

Laura thought she had better save the conversation about bits and saddles and crops (and gelding) for another day.

The next morning, dressed in comfy old jeans, a tee, muckers and gloves, Laura impatiently waited in the van for her mother. Armed with a travel mug full of strong coffee, Mrs. Connor drove while Laura chatted excitedly.

"I wonder how I'll do? I hope the horses all behave. You know, I never even asked what the job pays!"

Mrs. Connor travelled along the route she had decided was the safest and fastest for Laura to get to the farm by bicycle, should the need arise. Laura made careful mental note of the street signs and landmarks along the way.

Pulling up in the parking area, CeeCee turned to her daughter. Reaching into her windbreaker, she handed Laura a cellphone. Laura stared at it in surprise. "What's this?"

"Honey, I know we've dragged our feet about getting you one of these, but I think you could use one now. Especially if you're going to be working way out here in the boonies. We were going to give it to you for your birthday anyway. It's not super fancy. I think you can text and take pictures with it, but it's only to be used to call home when you need to be picked up, or in an emergency."

She reached over and powered the phone on. "See, all juiced up and ready to go. Home is the first number on speed dial."

Laura was speechless, but managed to croak, "Thanks, Mom. This is so cool, it's off the hook." She kissed her mother quickly on the cheek before hopping out of the van.

Mrs. Leeds was already in the barn, tending to the morning feed. Laura took a deep breath scented with horse smells and wood shavings.

"Where would you like me to start?" she asked.

"Oh, hello dear," Mrs. Leeds greeted her, looking up from a feed tub into which she was pouring a measure of vitamin supplements. She indicated the yellowish powder in the dispensing scoop. "A special broodmare potion for the mother-to-be," she said. "Wonderful stuff for building better babies."

The pair walked the length of the barn, Mrs. Leeds pointing out the notes jotted on small chalkboards outside each stall: Glory – 1 SF 2oz G 2F.

"Morning Glory gets one scoop of sweet feed, glucosamine, which is a joint supplement for her creaky old joints, and two flakes of hay."

She pointed to another note: Dudley – 1 SF 1 CO 3F.

"Dudley is 17 hands and gets lots of exercise, so he gets one scoop of sweet feed plus one scoop of crimped oats, and three flakes of hay."

Laura looked puzzled when she got to Smidge's stall: Smidge – SSW, 1/2 EX and 1F. She turned to Mrs. Leeds for a translation.

"Smidge is such a small pony that he really doesn't need any sweet feed, but he looks so sad while the others are having theirs that I feed him a tiny handful – a smidge." She laughed. "He also gets half a scoop of extruded hay pellets, which keeps him busy chewing and prevents him from getting bored. And we all know there's nothing worse than a bored pony."

Laura didn't know, but felt that she would find out, some day.

While the horses worked on their breakfast, creating a symphony of snuffling, chewing and bucket thumping, Mrs. Leeds went over the barn routine with Laura. There was a lot to remember: who got turned out in which paddock, where the stable tools were kept, the location of the manure pile, the list of emergency phone numbers.

Mrs. Leeds explained that each animal was given a visual once-over before and after turnout to check for cuts, bumps and swellings. "They can play pretty rough at times," she said, "but generally, everybody gets along."

She showed Laura the correct way to lead a horse to the field and reminded her always to turn the horse's head towards the gate before releasing the clip on the lead shank. "Less chance you'll get kicked, even by accident," Mrs. Leeds explained.

Laura took Phantom, Smidge and Glory to their respective paddocks without incident, then donned her work gloves for a lesson in Mucking Out 101. Mrs. Leeds showed her how to pile the reusable shavings to one side of the stall, shovel out the soggy spots and poo piles, and sift through the remains with the "apple picker" for stragglers. The student's favourite part by far was spreading clean, fragrant shavings around the stall.

Laura was left to finish the other five stalls while Mrs. Leeds busied herself sweeping down cobwebs and tidying the tack room and office. Laura's arms were aching by the third stall.

While she worked, Laura thought of Flash and wondered if he was behaving himself back at the house. His nose had been out of joint ever since she told him he could not go with her to the barn.

"Too risky," she had said.

"Rubbish," he had replied, and stalked off to sulk in the closet.

Laura's brain was swimming with information by the time they broke for lunch. The day was warm and sunny. Laura took her lunchbag to the picnic table under a huge elm where she could watch the horses while she ate. They did not bother to look up from their intent mowing of the early summer grass. The only exception was Alba, the broodmare, who pinned her ears occasionally and made ugly faces at Glory if she wandered too close.

"Crisps?" Mrs. Leeds placed a bowl of sour cream and onion potato chips on the table. She sat down with her sandwich and the two ate in silence, grateful for the break.

Phantom, the grey, lifted his head and stared intently at some unseen object in the distance. Mrs. Leeds followed Laura's gaze to the attractive animal. "He's a wonderful show hunter, 'A' Circuit material. His owner hopes to move him up to the big leagues this season."

She straightened suddenly. "Oh! How rude of me. You never asked about the wages. That's actually one of the things I liked about you," she said with a wink. "The pay is eight dollars per hour, six hours per day, Monday to Friday. If you would like to attend shows with us on the weekends, you're more than welcome. There's always room for an extra groom or gofer or horse-holder. I pay a small day fee of twenty-five dollars – not much, I know, but for a beginner, the learning experience is invaluable."

Laura quickly did the math in her head. Not counting the weekend work, she would be making over two hundred dollars per week. She supposed there would be taxes, but it seemed like a fortune. Suddenly, she wasn't the least bit tired anymore.

The remaining time of her shift she spent sweeping the aisles, scrubbing and refilling water buckets, and setting the evening feed.

"The horses stay out all day until five o'clock or so. They have lots of fresh water in the outdoor troughs, and run-in sheds for shade. We bring them in if the weather turns really nasty, or of course, if there's lightning."

Laura smiled and nodded. She totally understood the consequences of lightning.

It was a very tired and dirty – but happy – young girl who called her mother shortly after one o'clock on her new cellphone to say she was ready to come home. The van had barely rolled to a stop in the driveway at their house before Laura was out the door, bounding up the porch steps.

"Where are you off to in such a hurry?" her mother called after her.

I'm going to check on my talking, flying horse was what Laura wanted to say, but what she really said was, "I'm, aaah, stinky and really need a shower."

Flash was very happy to see his mistress. He sniffed her hands with great interest. "Hmmmmm, horses. And lady horses, too. Tell me all about your day."

Laura started to strip off her sweaty tee, then stopped with a little gasp. "Oh," she said, face reddening. "I can't undress with you watching. That's just too weird."

Flash snorted. "I think you've forgotten that I've lived in this room for years. Mind you, I did spend most of my time looking out the window."

Laura collected some clean clothes and headed, still dressed, to the bathroom for a much-needed shower.

CHAPTER 5

"I want to go to the barn," Flash complained petulantly as Laura prepared for her third day of work. "I promise I'll stay out of sight. I might even be of some use, you know, helping."

Laura sincerely doubted that Flash could a) stay hidden, and b) be of much help, but she was growing tired of his begging.

"All right already, I'll tell Mom that I want to ride my bike today. I bet she'd like to sleep in, anyway."

Tiptoeing into her parents' room, Laura told her mother her plans. CeeCee mumbled a weak protest, then gratefully pulled the covers over her head. "Thanks, sweetie. Be safe. Make sure you take your cellphone, and if you're tired after work, I'll be happy to come and get you."

With Flash safely tucked into her backpack, Laura wheeled her reliable old mountain bike out of the driveway. The summer sun was still low on the horizon, but its rays warmed Laura's bare arms.

Once they were clear of cars and houses, Laura and Flash struck up a conversation. Flash even flew beside her whenever the coast was clear, which was often at this early hour. He swooped and dove and nickered his funny little nicker.

Laura loved to see him so free and happy. She tried her best to get him outside as often as possible to graze and gallop and soar, but it wasn't always easy. Twice, her dad had walked unexpectedly into the backyard to work on their new garden shed, and Flash had been forced to dive for the bushes. It was nerve-wracking, but it was all she could do for the time being.

With a swoosh, Flash disappeared into the open backpack. A moment later, Laura heard crunching. "Hey, that's my apple!" she protested.

"Not anymore," came the slobbery reply.

Fortunately, Mrs. Leeds announced she had to run into town for supplies and would be gone for a couple of hours, leaving Laura alone with the chores.

"Are you certain you'll be okay?" the kindly owner asked once the horses were all safely in their paddocks.

"Absolutely!" Laura replied. "I'll be fine. Don't worry about us – I mean, me."

The farm truck was barely out of sight before Flash was in the air. He immediately headed for the paddocks to introduce himself to his fellow equines. Unfortunately, they were quite startled by his friendly, "Hello, everybody," and bolted wildly to the far side of their fields. Even brave little Smidge joined the stampede – not because he was afraid, but simply because everyone else was running. The herd stood against the far fence, snorting and blowing loudly, nostrils flared, eyes bulging, ears trained toward the tiny intruder.

"*Flash!*" Laura yelled. Flash was about to launch himself toward his new-found, terrified friends, but the anger in the girl's voice stopped him. "Get back here!"

"But…but…I want to speak to them." Flash looked beseechingly back and forth between the seething Laura and the skittery herd. His wings drooped and he slunk sullenly along the top rail of the fence, back to his livid mistress.

Laura strode back to the barn, muttering under her breath. Flash fluttered behind her swinging ponytail. From the barn door, Laura watched as the horses uneasily moved apart and began grazing again.

"I'm sorry," Flash began, "I had no idea they would react like that."

"It's okay," Laura said, her annoyance fading when she saw how genuinely crushed he was.

"It's just that I was so excited to see my own kind again, even if they are more like distant relatives." He looked longingly towards the paddocks.

"I promise I'll make proper introductions soon. You really have to take things slowly where horses are concerned, you know."

"The horses of *my* day were much more friendly and relaxed," Flash observed, tossing his mane.

"The horses of *your* day ran free and may have been happier," Laura shot back. "But they probably had worms and got eaten by wild animals on a regular basis."

True to her word, once the bulk of the barn chores were done, Laura perched the little horse in the crook of her elbow and escorted him back to the paddocks. Immediately, all heads were raised, but the pair's casual approach did not incite a stampede this time.

Laura had already decided that Smidge was the perfect candidate for the initial meeting, as he was rarely ruffled by anything. "Absolutely bombproof," was how Mrs. Leeds described him. The little black pony came over to the fence at Laura's bidding, sniffing her outstretched hand. Flash watched quietly from his perch on Laura's arm, then cautiously began to make his way along her forearm, keeping his wings pinned against his sides to prevent spooking Smidge and setting off another riot.

Smidge poked his little muzzle through the gap

in the boards. Flash stretched his neck forward to touch noses, the time-honoured equine greeting.

Carefully, the winged visitor stepped off Laura's arm onto the fence rail. She was relieved about that, as his tiny, sharp hooves dug into her skin, and he was a lot heavier than he looked.

And so began a dialogue and a friendship. Flash alternated between a low *huh huh huh* nickering and quiet human talk, but slipped into a strange combination of the two that Smidge actually seemed to understand. At the end of the exchange, the pony nodded his head up and down enthusiastically as if in agreement with something Flash had imparted to him.

"He is going to explain to the rest of the horses that there is no reason to be afraid of me," he said. "I thought that would be the best–" He broke off suddenly, staring down the driveway. Mrs Leeds was back!

Laura had nowhere to hide Flash, but Smidge, sensing their panic, shook his considerable shock of thick pony mane, and Flash, without a moment's hesitation, straddled his neck. Laura hastily fluffed up the unruly, coarse hair to hide him. The result was a perfectly normal-looking pony with an extra pair of wide eyes peering out from the forelock between his ears.

With a furtive glance behind her, Laura was off down the driveway to help Mrs. Leeds unload the supplies. As she couldn't sling the heavy sacks of oats and sweet feed over her shoulder like the strong older woman, she improvised by sliding them off the tailgate of the truck and into a waiting wheelbarrow, where she carted them two at a time to the feed room.

Mrs. Leeds was impressed with her ingenuity. "It doesn't matter how you get it there, as long as it gets there," she said with approval.

At the end of the day, Laura hefted her backpack over her shoulder and casually walked over to Smidge's paddock to say goodbye to the horses. Smidge waited patiently by the fence, his hitchhiker still in place.

"I'm going to turn around. Get in quick while Mrs. Leeds isn't looking," Laura hissed to Flash. He obediently scrambled from his pony-hair hiding place to the depths of the backpack.

On the way home, the pair actually laughed about the close call, and Laura began to feel that life with Flash could be normal. Well, almost normal.

Chapter 6

"We're going to a model show!"

Krissy made this announcement as she flopped onto the patio swing on Laura's back deck. "We haven't been to one in ages. There's a show and sale in the city at the convention centre this weekend." She waved a section of the newspaper at her friend in case proof was needed.

"It's about time you had a good idea," Laura teased. "We could take the bus up after I finish work on Friday. Cool."

At one time Laura had shown her models, and enjoyed the fun, friendly competition. She found, however, that lately, it was becoming harder to spend the time and money necessary to "rework" models or purchase new ones in order to stay really competitive. As an avid collector, though, she could not resist attending shows whenever she had the chance.

"I'm going with you!" Flash insisted when he caught wind of the girls' plans.

Laura chewed thoughtfully on her lip. Her first instinct was to say no, but Flash had been accompanying her and Krissy on many of their outings recently without any major disasters.

"Okay," she agreed, " but you'll have to–"

"I know, I know," Flash sighed. "I'll have to stay out of sight and do whatever you say. I am aware of the rules, you understand."

If only you would obey them, Laura thought ruefully.

Krissy's mother picked Laura up at her house after work on Friday as planned. Hastily showered, hair still damp and her first paycheck tucked into the pocket of her jeans, Laura asked if she and Krissy could be dropped off in front of the bank in town. "I need to deposit my cheque and take out some money for the show." The very words sounded strange and grown-up. "We can walk to the bus stop from there."

The pocketful of cash felt very good against Laura's hip as the city-bound bus pulled away from the curb. Laura rearranged the backpack – the "Flashpack," as the girls had dubbed it – so that the tiny traveller wouldn't be squashed or suffocated.

Even with his limited view from the confines of the bag, Flash found the trip very exciting: all the passengers, the swaying motion of the bus, the world whizzing by outside the windows. A couple of times he lost control and let out a tiny horsey squeal, much to the girls' horror.

Curious glances directed their way prompted Laura to lean over and whisper "Knock it off!" at the hidden troublemaker.

The convention centre was bustling with model enthusiasts and their entries. Long tables displayed hundreds of exhibits in categories such as Custom

Model and Original Finish. There were also halter classes for Andalusians, ponies and Appaloosas, beautiful Arabians in costume, and even models set in elaborate racetrack, show ring and desert scenes. Laura sighed happily at the sight.

Near the entrance, she spotted some people she recognized. Taylor and Tyler, or The Terrible Twins as they were known on the local model circuit, were a year younger than Laura, but tons of fun. They had always gone out of their way to help her at model shows, sharing their tips and tricks.

While Laura caught up on the latest gossip with the twosome, she rested the heavy backpack on an empty corner of a nearby table. Top-heavy, as its occupant was standing on his hind legs inside, trying to look out, the bag fell over with a *whoomp.* Flash tumbled out, end over end, onto the table. Exposed for all to see, he immediately froze – one foreleg raised as if about to paw or strike, wings sleek and motionless.

It was several moments before Tyler's gaze drifted to the figure on the table. "Holy crap!" he exclaimed. "Where in the world did you get that?"

Both Krissy and Laura's heads snapped around

in unison. *Oh God,* Laura thought, heart sinking.

Flash remained immobile, but oh so visible. He may as well have had a spotlight on him and a flashing red beacon strapped to his head.

"It's fabulous!" Taylor squealed, and lunged to pick up the statue. Her expression changed the second she wrapped her hand around his midsection. "Oh!" She immediately dropped him and pulled back, startled. "It's warm…and furry… and weird."

"It's, ahhh, a new type of material. Very lifelike, don't you think?" Laura said nervously. She was stunned at Flash's irresponsible act. He had landed back on the table with a soft *clunk* and remained on his side, unmoving.

Krissy made the first move, scooping up the winged figure, stuffing him hastily into the backpack and moving off down the aisle. "Well, gotta go. So much to see, so little time, you know."

Laura followed her friend, offering apologies to the twins over her shoulder.

Across the aisle, a pair of dark eyes watched the girls retreat. *That was no model,* thought the boy, who had witnessed the entire scene. He recognized

Laura and Krissy from other model shows. He lived in the same town as they did, and even attended the same school, but he was very, very different from the carefree young girls. While he envisioned his own existence as tragic and full of darkness, he imagined those two spoiled brats as living charmed lives, and hated them for it.

Blade, the name he had adopted, lived in the older section of town, where modest winterized cottages served as homes for some of the lower-income families. The lanky thirteen-year-old kept mostly to himself, playing war games online, reading graphic novels, and listening to goth music: AFI, Skinny Puppy, Wumpscut. Mostly, he tried to stay out of his father's way. The man did not understand his son's sullen withdrawal, body piercings or choice of clothes and music. After a night of drinking, he would often verbally and physically challenge the boy.

Blade did have one genuine passion: medieval artifacts. He was fascinated with books, games, artwork and models depicting knights and battles during the Dark Ages. The medieval jousting model classes had attracted his interest, which explained his attendance at the show, even though he generally believed that people who collected and showed stupid plastic horses were losers.

Blade was now quite certain – no, he was *positive* – that he had just seen Pegasus fall out of a backpack and strike a pose. He had no idea what it was or where it came from, but he knew he had to possess it.

He started down the aisle after the girls.

One of the hits of the show, to Laura's delight, was the Breyer Pegasus model. A crowd had formed around the display in the merchandising section.

"Oh," Laura breathed. "I'd love to have one of those!"

"What on earth for?" The muffled question emanated from her backpack. "You already have *me.*"

"Shhh!" Laura said through clenched teeth. "You're already in deep do-do. Besides, it would be company for you. Maybe I'll save up and get one at the end of the summer."

"*Pfffft.*" Flash, disgusted, made a rude noise and fell silent.

Two hours later, with packages in hand, the girls tumbled happily out of the building and into a waiting bus. The door hinged shut, then opened again to admit a tall, dark-haired boy. He slouched into a seat near the back, where he had a clear view of the girls through the shock of black hair hanging over his smouldering eyes. He stared intently at the pair, causing them to giggle nervously and look away.

"Who's the creepy goth kid?" asked Krissy out of the corner of her mouth.

"I dunno. He goes to our school, but he's a grade ahead. He was in my 7/8 math class. Calls himself Blood or Blade or something weird. Maybe he's a stalker."

The pair soon forgot about their watcher and spent the rest of the trip home chatting about the show, Laura's job and the prospects for avoiding boredom for the rest of the summer. As they stood by the back doors of the bus, waiting for it to slow to a stop, Laura said, "Hey, I nearly forgot. Mrs. Leeds asked me to work the horse show at the fairgrounds this Sunday. Do you wanna come? Banbury Cross is taking two horses. It'll be fun."

Without taking his gaze off the floor, Blade smiled. *The fairgrounds on Sunday*, he thought. *I'll see you there, girls. Be sure to bring your little friend.*

Chapter 7

Laura could not believe how much work went into attending a horse show. The bathing, grooming, clipping, braiding, leg and tail wrapping, packing and trailering were very time-consuming, but still fun. The jittery nerves of Phantom's and Dudley's owners were very apparent, even though they joked and laughed and tried to look cool and collected.

The grey gelding was entered in the hunter classes, two on the flat and two over fences, while Dudley, the event horse, would be using the jumper classes as a tune-up for his first horse trial later in the season.

The Banbury Cross crew arrived early at the fairgrounds. The grass was still heavy with dew and the air was cool, although fiercely high temperatures were forecast for later in the day.

"Hopefully, we can get in and get out before the heat gets too brutal," Mrs. Leeds said cheerfully as she applied a final coating of hoof polish to Phantom's feet.

Laura had argued with Flash for two days that it was too risky to let him come to the horse show. He had looked so pitiful and dejected that she had finally relented. "Well, as long as you *really* behave this time. No stunts like at the model fair. Promise?"

Flash promised.

And he did behave – at first. He hid behind a hay bale on the storage shelf in the front of the trailer, where he could safely look through one of the louvered vents on either side. But he quickly grew bored, and it became very warm in the enclosed space as the sun beat down on the open field which served as a parking lot.

Once the entourage of girls and horses left for the show ring, Flash decided it was safe to come out of hiding. He peered out the back of the empty trailer, was satisfied that no one was watching, and fluttered to the limb of a nearby tree. The shade and slight breeze were a welcome respite from the muggy warmth of the trailer.

Flash's movement was witnessed, however, by the same pair of jealous dark eyes that had watched his antics at the convention centre. Blade, looking quite out of place in his long black coat, black jeans, piercings and clunky silver jewellery, had been wandering among the parked trucks and trailers, searching for some logo or lettering identifying Banbury Cross Stables. He had just spotted the bright red pickup when Flash's departure caught his eye.

From his perch in the elm tree, Flash spied some sweet feed which had been spilled in the grass beside the trailer. Folding his wings, he swooped down and began to devour the tasty treat, unaware of the danger lurking nearby.

Blade slunk stealthily along the far side of the Banbury Cross trailer while Flash, totally engrossed in his snack, took no notice. He was startled when the fishnet Blade had concealed under his coat fell around him like a shroud. His first reaction was to flee upward, but the escape route was blocked by netting. He succeeded only in tangling the tips of his strong wings in the unyielding mesh.

The net was flipped over, and Flash was now on his back, legs flailing, while Blade reached carefully inside, trying to avoid the kicking hooves and snapping teeth as the little horse fought for his life. The boy finally got a secure grip on his captive's midsection, then hoisted him out of the net and into a waiting drawstring bag which he quickly sealed shut.

Flash was in despair. Inside the bag it was pitch dark and smelled like feet. His wings were aching from trying to break free. Blade was moving now, and Flash was being bumped with every one of the boy's long strides. The movement, the fear and the smell were making him nauseated, but he tried to keep his thoughts clear. He heard the voice of the announcer over the PA system getting louder and realized they were approaching the front gate. He was being kidnapped, and there was nothing he could do about it.

"HELP!" he shrieked in his loudest voice. "*HELP ME!!*"

The movement stopped abruptly and the bag

dropped to the ground. The drawstring loosened, and as daylight flooded into the bag, Flash saw his chance. He burst upward through the small opening and past the awestruck Blade, who was in shock from the sound of the voice that had come from the sack.

"It can talk?!" he yelped.

Flash rocketed straight upwards, trying to put as much distance between himself and the boy, while scanning the area for some sort of cover. Luckily, the incident had not drawn any attention, as most eyes were focused on the action in the show ring.

Flash landed on the flat roof of a nearby utility shed and ducked behind the outer edge, heart beating so loudly he felt sure his would-be kidnapper could hear it. Blade paced back and forth wildly, looking upward, eyes squinting against the sun, and cursing loudly.

The second of the over-fences hunter classes was finally wrapping up. Phantom had produced two spectacular rounds, winning the first class and appearing to have the second one well in hand. They had earned ribbons in both flat classes as well. The championship was within reach – a very successful day for his owner, Kerry-Lynn.

Before the winners were pinned, Laura and Krissy headed for the trailers to make sure that fresh water and a full haynet were waiting for the gelding when he returned. Laura sensed that something wasn't right as soon as they reached the parked rig. A single, silvery white feather lay in the grass. She wrenched open the man-door at the front of the trailer and peered inside. It took a second for her eyes to adjust to the dim interior.

"Flash?" she said, voice wavering, and then, panicking. "*Flash?*"

There was no reply.

"*Pssssst.*" The soft, sibilant sound came from behind and above Laura.

She spun, looking up. At first she could not see the small form standing precariously on a high tree limb. "Flash! What are you doing up there?"

Flash glanced left and right, eyeing his surroundings nervously. "It was that boy. That *awful* boy. He tried to steal me, but I managed to escape."

"What boy?" Laura asked, chest tightening with fear. "*What boy!?*"

Flash decided it was safe enough to come down from his high perch. He landed on the trailer fender. "I don't know where he came from, but he trapped me in some sort of net and placed me in a dreadful, smelly bag."

Laura crouched down and inspected the little horse at eye level. He looked dishevelled, but otherwise uninjured – "Like he was rode hard and put away wet," as her mother liked to say.

"How did you escape, exactly?" Laura asked.

Flash avoided her gaze. "I, uh, outsmarted him."

"Outsmarted him how?" Laura was getting annoyed at his evasiveness, but was equally sure she wasn't going to like the answer.

"I called for help, and I guess it startled him–"

"You *spoke* in front of this person?" Laura was horrified. "Do you realize what this means?"

Krissy stepped in to diffuse the tension. "What did this boy look like, the one who kidnapped you?"

Flash fluffed his sore wings. "He was dark-haired and very pale, and had some sort of shiny ring through his eyebrow. He was dressed all in black and wore a long black coat."

The girls looked at each other. "The scary kid on the bus!" they said in unison.

Approaching voices snapped the trio back to the present. Flash darted back to his hiding place in the trailer, while the girls scrambled to fill Phantom's haynet. Gabrielle and Dudley walked in from the other direction, returning from the warm-up ring.

For the next forty-five minutes the girls were totally absorbed. Phantom had to be washed down and cooled out, while the big bay warmblood, prior to his trip to the jumper ring, needed a final wipe-down, coat of hoof polish and mouth de-slobbering, a task Krissy found particularly disgusting.

Flash promised to stay hidden, and this time he was so frightened and frazzled that Laura actually believed him. She fetched a cupful of water for the little guy before she and Krissy went back to the show ring. She was certain he must be thirsty after his ordeal.

Dudley did not fare quite as well as his stablemate in the jumper classes. He seemed strong and unruly in the three-foot class, pulling poor Gabrielle's arms out of their sockets as he hauled her around the ring. In response, she schooled him mercilessly between classes. The result was a listless and sloppy second trip, with two rails down.

Gabrielle was discouraged, but still managed to smile and pat Dudley's sweaty brown neck. "Oh well," she sighed. "My bad. Cross-country's always been his best phase anyway."

Worried that the goth kid would return to cause more trouble, Laura and Krissy constantly scanned the crowd at ringside and for anyone wandering near the trailers, until they were satisfied he had fled the showgrounds.

It was an exhausted and grimy troupe that pulled into the stableyard at Banbury Cross. Laura had never felt so bone-weary in her life. She desperately needed a shower to rinse off the layer of sticky show dust that seemed to cling to every square inch of her body.

Once the horses were all squared away in their stalls with fresh hay and their tendons tingling with astringent wash, Laura placed a call to her mother to come and retrieve her and Krissy.

"Well, you've really done it this time," Laura admonished Flash. They were waiting under a tree near the end of the driveway, enjoying the shade and what little breeze stirred. "What if this kid tells someone about the Amazing Flying Talking Horse?"

"Pardon me," Flash replied calmly, "but what makes you think that anyone would believe a far-fetched story like that?"

Laura considered this. Perhaps Flash was right. Trying to convince someone you had witnessed something so completely incredible, without a stitch of actual proof, would be very difficult indeed.

Krissy agreed. "If anyone ever asks, we have to deny everything, even if it means, well, stretching the truth."

Laura winced. She hated lying, yet seemed to be doing a lot of it lately.

"But in the meantime," Krissy continued brightly, "you've got to stay out of trouble, you little monkey."

Flash looked petulant, but wisely remained silent.

That evening found Laura watching television with her parents, while upstairs Flash stretched out comfortably on a makeshift nest of old baby blankets in her closet between the running shoes and abandoned Barbies. Neither was aware of the shadowy figure across the street watching the house intently with bitter, narrowed eyes.

Chapter 8

Partway through the week Mrs. Leeds suggested that, if she was interested, Laura could saddle up Glory and give her a little light exercise in the outdoor arena after chores. Laura was excited – and a bit apprehensive. Her riding experience was quite limited, and she didn't want to look clumsy or inept in front of her employer.

Mrs. Leeds sensed her hesitation. "Don't worry, dear, I'll be here to help you and give you some pointers, if you like."

Laura liked very much.

Although Morning Glory was retired from the

breeding shed, her owner still liked to ride her occasionally. "Keeps her from getting pudgy and bored," she said. "Besides, I think she likes the attention."

Glory was pretty much the only horse at the farm that Laura *could* ride. Smidge, although he was a sweetheart, was too short even for Laura's small frame. Alba was in foal, and Psycho was, well, too psycho for an unskilled novice.

"One day I'm certain you'll even be able to take Bates Motel out for a spin," Mrs. Leeds said encouragingly.

Laura thought that *spin* was the operative word in that sentence, as she watched the chestnut gelding bucking and squealing in his field.

The session on Glory was nearly perfect. The old mare started out a bit stiffly, but soon her old joints warmed up and she began to move with fluid ease. Laura was delighted at the smoothness of her gaits and the responsiveness to her timid aids. They worked at the walk, trot and easy canter both ways around the ring, and by the end of the half hour Laura felt more confident and capable than she had in her life.

Laura and Krissy were now in the habit of taking a walk just before sunset in order to let Flash have an airborne romp in the park under the cover of approaching darkness. The evening air was pleasantly cool on this particular evening as the girls strolled down the boulevard, the ever-present pink backpack slung over Laura's shoulder. They settled into swings in the deserted playground and chattered idly until it was dark enough to free Flash. He exploded from the bag with a swoosh and careered through the trees to the end of the park, then slalomed back through the line of lamp posts. They were more decorative than illuminating, casting only a minimal light. The girls figured that, even if he was spotted by a passerby, he would likely be mistaken for an owl or a mockingbird.

Laura let Flash stretch his wings and enjoy himself until it was time to head home. She uttered a quick, sharp whistle, and he responded immediately, alighting on her outstretched arm like a hunting falcon, then stepping carefully into the zippered abyss.

"Just how long do you plan to keep that thing a secret?"

The sudden, unexpected voice behind them caused the girls to gasp and whirl around. A figure stepped out of the shadows by the boundary hedge.

"You!" Laura cried accusingly. "You're the one who stole Flash!" She instinctively, foolishly, moved toward the boy, fists clenched and raised.

For all his cool detachment and hostile demeanor, Blade looked uncertain – even frightened – for a moment.

Laura saw the look in his eyes and stopped, lowering her hands. "Why did you do that? You could have hurt him!"

Blade had regained some of his bravado. "You shouldn't keep that thing all to yourself, you know. You could make a lot of money selling it or putting it in a zoo or something."

Laura again looked as though she would be quite happy to strike the smirking boy. "Flash is not a thing, he's a him and he's made of flesh and bone… and feathers. And he's not for sale. He'll never be for sale and if you ever come near him again you'll be really sorry." She stared at Blade coldly.

Blade shifted his weight nervously from foot to foot. "I'll tell people about him–"

"Go ahead!" Laura shouted. "Nobody'll believe you anyway, you freak!" She regretted the words as soon as they were out of her mouth. She had never said an unkind word to anyone, but this dark and forbidding boy needed to be set straight. She spun on her heel and stalked across the park.

Krissy gawked at her friend's outburst, then trotted to catch up, casting nervous glances over her shoulder at Blade, who remained motionless near the swings.

"Holy cow!" she exclaimed when they were back on the boulevard. "You really kicked his butt!"

The colour in Laura's flushed cheeks was fading and she looked as though she was about to cry. "He's right, you know," she said sadly. "Someone, someday, is going to find out about Flash and everything will change."

Laura had trouble sleeping that night. Flash sensed her despair and fluttered to her side on the bed. He nuzzled her hand with his soft muzzle, his warm breath leaving little moist patches on her skin.

"May I say something?" Flash asked quietly.

"Sure, and sorry I've been so bummed."

"This is the conclusion I have reached. I think that awful boy has a point. You could become quite wealthy by displaying me around the country, or perhaps on the television machine. Maybe even *Animal Planet.* You say your parents are struggling to make ends meet. I could be the answer to your family's financial problems."

"Oh, Flash." Laura hugged him to her chest. "That is so sweet, but I could never do that. Not ever. It's not about money. It would be a terrible life for you, always being stared at and forced to perform."

"And travelling and meeting people and being able to fly in the sunlight in the middle of the day. Yes, that would be terrible." He looked at her sideways, a twinkle in his eye.

Laura placed him gently on the covers in front of her. "Seriously, I don't want to talk about this anymore. Go to sleep."

They slept.

CHAPTER 9

Laura rode Morning Glory three times that week. She absorbed as much information as possible from Mrs. Leeds during each session, paying close attention to every pointer and quickly learning that when something felt right, it usually was right. She was exhilarated after each lesson and couldn't wait for the next opportunity to ride the chestnut mare. Glory may not have been very exciting, but she was perfect for Laura, and the young girl was growing to love and trust her.

After Friday's lesson, Laura was allowed to take Glory out of the ring and into one of the large hayfields behind the barn.

"Stay to the edge where the grass is worn and keep her to a walk or slow trot. Twice around will be fine – poor old Glory doesn't get out much anymore, so this will be fun for her, too," Mrs. Leeds said.

Laura decided it would be best only to trot while heading away from the barn and walk once she'd passed the halfway point in the field. *Much safer,* she thought.

With the warm sun on their backs, the pair trotted off through the lush alfalfa and clover. It smelled wonderful, and Laura couldn't imagine a day more perfect. She posted to the smooth rise and fall of the mare's trotting stride, concentrating on soft, following hands and a long, secure leg. *Head up, heels down, straight line from bit to elbow,* she recited in her head.

It was during the second circuit of the field that things started to unravel. She had trotted farther than she had planned, past the halfway mark and then some, and the thoroughbred was getting a little quick.

Close your fingers, sink your weight into your seat, open your body angle, she remembered. Except it wasn't working. The mare continued to lengthen her stride into a ground-eating trot. Suddenly, a grouse exploded from the long grass beside the trail, and they were off.

Laura clutched wildly at the reins, seesawing frantically and trying to remember what she had been taught about stopping a runaway. The mare had settled into a dead run and was still following the trail in a straight line, so there was little chance of Laura falling off – for now.

The frightened, over-horsed girl was attempting a pulley rein by anchoring one hand against Glory's neck and pulling up and back with the other rein – to little avail. She was neither strong enough nor aggressive enough to accomplish this desperate act, and they were quickly approaching the turnoff to the barn.

Whooosh!

Something sailed past Laura's head. It was Flash.

"Stop her!" Laura shrieked.

Flash flew ahead of the mare, blocking her path, then gradually slowed his pace. The mare, ears forward, followed suit until she was back to a bouncy trot. From there, Laura was able to rein her in.

"Are you all right?" Flash asked, concerned. He

flitted around Glory's head. "*Bad* mare."

Glory snorted loudly.

"Are you all right?"

This was not an echo, but Mrs. Leeds' worried shout from the edge of the field. Flash quickly departed to the cover of the nearby trees.

"Meet me at the backpack," Laura said out of the side of her mouth.

The stable owner was extremely upset about the incident and apologized profusely. "You poor dear, I'm so sorry. I had no idea Glory would bolt like that. She's usually unflappable."

"It's not her fault, really. It was a grouse or pheasant or something that spooked her. I'm okay, for real." Laura undid her helmet and shook out her hair.

"Funny, I could have sworn I saw a big silver bird flying around you when you stopped. Did you see it?" Mrs. Leeds looked puzzled.

Laura had not realized that the woman had witnessed so much of Flash's rescue. "Uh…I think it was just a seagull. Funny, huh? Scared by a grouse and saved by a seagull."

"Yes, very odd indeed," Mrs. Leeds mused.

True to his word, Flash had made his way back to the barn and was tucked into his backpack by the time Laura was ready to leave. Mrs. Leeds continued offering apologies, which Laura, waiting impatiently for her mother to pick her up, persisted in waving off.

She was anxious to get home. Her parents were hosting one of their famous summer pot-luck barbeques and she wanted to help with the preparations. She liked her parents' friends. Most were musicians and it was inevitable that an impromptu jam session would break out. Wisely, the neighbours were invited as well, and no one had ever complained about the noise.

Flash was tucked away in Laura's room with an extra-special dinner of oatmeal cookies and a handful of sweet feed filched from the feed room at the barn. Laura had planted grass seed in a large clay pot on the windowsill so that Flash could nibble on fresh greenery whenever he wanted. She had told her mother it was for the cat. "Maxi really likes it,

Mom, except when she eats too much and yaks on the floor."

Oddly, Maxi and Flash had actually become friends after their initial stormy meeting. Laura would often find them curled up together in the closet on Flash's baby blanket nest, Maxi purring loudly, Flash snoring.

This night, Laura threw the windows open wide so that Flash could enjoy the sights and sounds of the party. She stroked his neck and ran her fingers along his strong wings. "You did good today, Flash. Thanks."

Flash bowed his head sheepishly and gave Laura his best "aw, gosh" look.

Friends and neighbours began arriving around seven-thirty and mingled on the Connors' spacious back deck, which was brightly lit with wonderfully tacky patio lanterns and tall tiki torches. There seemed to be a never-ending parade of food coming from the grill and the kitchen. Hamburgers, steaks, shrimp kabobs and a table laden with every conceivable type of salad greeted the hungry guests.

Krissy, who had just arrived with her parents, eyed the spread greedily and said, "It's like an all-you-can-eat barf-ay," as she scooped up a huge handful of taco chips. After making cheerful small talk to all the grownups – "Yes, I'm nearly thirteen now," and "I love your hair," and "Your daughter Sarah's on my soccer team" – Laura and Krissy helped themselves to heaping plates of food. They stole around to the front porch where it was quieter and they could talk freely without being overheard.

Krissy listened with widening eyes while Laura told of her harrowing near-disaster with Glory and Flash's quick thinking.

"That's so awesome," Krissy gushed. "But what about Mrs. Leeds? Didn't she see him?"

"Well, yes and no," Laura explained. "I convinced her he was just a seagull."

The conversation turned to Laura's birthday, which was now only three days away. As the girls ate and talked, an unwelcome but increasingly familiar figure appeared in the glow of the streetlight across the road. It was Blade, shuffling slowly along with his head down. Even from where the girls sat, they could tell that the boy was dejected. He looked up and stopped.

Laura hesitated only a second. "Hey kid, come over here."

Krissy looked at her like she'd gone mad.

"It's okay. I promise I won't beat you up," Laura called out again. The boy looked confused and hesitant, but crossed the street and approached the pair slowly.

"What's up?" It was less of a question than a peace offering.

Laura put her plate down and stood up. "Let's start over, okay? My name is Laura Connor and this is Krissy Martineau. Your name is actually Todd, right? I know it's not really Blade, 'cause you were in one of my classes last semester."

The boy looked decidedly off balance at this sudden change of heart. He had expected a confrontation. It would have been the second one so far that evening. Laura was startled to see a darkening on his left cheek when the light from the streetlamp fell across it. A bruise? She thought so. Something was clearly not right in this boy's life. Laura felt a twinge of something – concern, or perhaps pity, much to her surprise. Just hours before, she would have gladly clouted him herself, even though it was totally against her nature.

As if reading her mind, Todd/Blade squared his shoulders. "It's okay. It's just my dad... let's just say I'm better off out of his sight and his reach when he's gettin' his swerve on."

Once the meaning set in, Laura was horrified. She could never imagine her own parents raising a hand to her. "Hey," she said suddenly. "Do you want something to eat? There's tons of food." Before Todd could answer, she was through the screen door and running through the house.

She returned a couple of minutes later with a plate heaping with potato salad, barbequed shrimp and a fresh, thick hamburger. "I didn't know what you wanted on your burger, so I put everything on it. You can pick off what you don't want." She handed him a plastic knife and fork.

Todd took the plate after only a moment's hesitation. He sank down on the step and began to eat slowly, carefully, and then ravenously. Laura wondered how long it had been since he'd last had a decent meal.

The girls picked at their nearly empty plates just to be polite while Todd ate. When he was done, he wiped his mouth on his sleeve. He smiled shyly at Laura, who could not believe how such a simple facial expression could completely change how a person looked. Instead of surly and unfriendly, he actually looked, well, kinda cute.

"Thanks, that was really great. You're really lucky, you know. To have all this, I mean." With a wave of his hand, he indicated their modest but comfortable house with happy sounds coming from the backyard.

He's right, Laura thought. *We may not be rich, but I'm a very lucky girl.*

Chapter 10

Todd was the first to broach the subject that was hanging like a shroud over the trio on the porch.

"Look, I'm sorry about everything, stealing your Pegasus and all. I promise I won't try it again, and you're right, it would be stupid to tell anyone about it, 'cause they'd just think I was high or making it up. It's just that I'm really into fantasy and stuff, and he's so cool, you know, I just wanted–"

"Forget it," Laura interrupted. "Really."

"I'd really like to talk to him. I mean, he really does *talk*, right? It wasn't my imagination?"

Laura smiled widely. "Yeah, he really does talk.

Too much, sometimes." She briefly explained about the storm and how Flash came to life.

"That's so wild. Just imagine the stuff he's seen and the stories he could tell." Todd was genuinely excited, his eyes shining. "Do you think...would it be possible to meet him sometime?"

After rolling it over in her mind, Laura replied, "I think that's entirely up to Flash."

"Absolutely not!" Flash declared vehemently when Laura posed the question several hours later. She and Krissy had retreated upstairs for a moment while the band set up out back.

Todd had left shortly after their truce on the porch, promising to return the next day for the verdict. "If that was okay," he had quickly added.

Laura had assured him that it was.

Flash, however, was not at all happy about the prospect of another meeting with "that dreadful boy," as he referred to Todd. "Nothing good will come of it," he warned, stamping his hoof angrily. "Mark my words."

Laura did not agree with Flash's dire predictions. In fact, she was beginning to change her mind about Todd. While on the outside, he appeared to be a dangerous, brooding rebel, she now realized that inside, he was just a lost and lonely boy with a miserable home life.

It took a lot of persuading, but Flash finally gave in. "My fate is in your hands," he said, bowing dramatically, but his eyes showed no signs of humour.

"Ohhhh," Krissy groaned, rolling over and squinting against the harsh sunlight streaming through the curtains. "It can't be morning already."

"I'm afraid it is, girls," said Mrs. Connor from the doorway. She looked amazingly fresh considering the music and partying had gone on well into the wee hours. "If you two want breakfast, you'd better think about rising and shining."

"I might rise, but I'm not too sure about the shining part," Laura muttered from under the covers.

The smell of bacon wafting up the stairs did the trick. As the girls yawned and stretched, Flash trotted out of his closet haven. He was closely followed by Maxi, who rubbed against his side, nearly knocking him over with her furry bulk. "Cats," Flash sniffed in mock disgust. "So, when do I get to meet Mr. Personality?"

Laura laughed. "His name is Todd and I think he's coming over this afternoon."

As promised, Todd did show up right after lunch. It was a very different boy who stood on the porch on this day. At Laura's request, his signature black clothes were replaced by a pair of faded jeans and a simple white t-shirt, and his unruly black hair was combed back off his face. Gone was the black eyeliner, although the eyebrow ring was still in place. Laura thought she detected the slightest touch of concealer over the bruised cheek, but it was barely noticeable.

"Hi!" she greeted him lightly. "You look really great."

Todd looked embarrassed, but grinned shyly.

"You have to meet my mom and dad," Laura said. "They're on their way out shopping, but no one is allowed in the house unless they've inspected them first."

The meeting was awkward, as Todd had few social skills to speak of, but he did his best to be polite to her parents. Before they walked out the door, Mrs. Connor pulled her daughter aside. "He's an odd one. Not like the rest of your friends. Kind of strange and a bit spooky. Are you sure he's okay? How old is he?"

"I'm positive, Mom. He's thirteen and he's just been going through a tough time lately. We're only going to hang out back for a bit and finish cleaning up from the party, so don't worry."

Her mother sighed. "All right then. I have my cell on me if you need to call. For any reason." She glanced toward Todd, who was pretending to inspect their new garden shed. With a kiss and a wave, she was gone.

Laura retrieved Flash from his upstairs hideaway and carried him out to a secluded part of the backyard. She placed him in the empty bird bath, where he looked up quizzically at the open-mouthed Todd. "Wow," the astounded boy breathed. "Can I touch him?"

Flash tensed a bit as Todd's hand caressed his wings and back, but he did not protest.

"Say something."

Flash looked at Todd. "Oh help, I've been stuffed in a smelly bag and kidnapped by a dreadful boy… How's that?"

"Flash!" Laura admonished. "Don't be rude."

"What are you planning to do with him?" Todd asked, unaffected by the snub.

"Do with him? Nothing." Laura shrugged. "He's welcome to stay with me as long as he likes. It's not like I own him or anything. He's free to leave at any time."

Flash was a bit hurt by her breezy reply, but at the same time thought it very decent of her not to think of him as property.

Todd was full of questions: "Where did you come from? Are there others like you? Were there monsters? How did they die? What were the battles like?"

Flash answered each as best he could, glancing often at Laura for guidance and assurance. She finally ended the friendly interrogation about an hour later, leaving Flash free to flit about the garden. He plucked a fresh pea pod off the vine and took it to a shady spot, where he munched noisily on its green goodness.

Before Todd left, Laura and Krissy swore him to absolute secrecy. "I typed up an agreement that we all have to sign," Laura said.

She went up to her room and retrieved the document she had created and printed that morning. She was quite proud of the wording. Thanks to her dictionary and thesaurus it sounded very mature and legal. It read:

> *We the undersigned agree to never reveal the whereabouts of, nor admit to the existence of, the two-hand-high flying talking Pegasus commonly known as Flash. Failure to obey the terms of this pact will result in expulsion from the group and loss of contact with said Flash, and other possible punishment yet to be decided.*

"We need a name for this pact," Krissy said.

Laura thought for a moment. "We'll call ourselves the Turtle Creek Triad," she announced. "I read where a triad was a group of three people with something in common... I think. Anyway, it sounds cool."

The others agreed. Todd thought they should seal the bond in blood, but the girls thought the old "blood brother" ritual of mashing punctured thumbs together was just too gross. They finally agreed to prick their thumbs with a pin and each leave a fingerprint on the printed pact, which they also signed. As an afterthought, Flash dipped a hoof in the muddy earth under the bird bath and applied his mark to the top of the paper. It all looked very official and powerful – like something not even the darkest magic could destroy.

July 17th dawned grey and gloomy, but Laura didn't care if it was snowing gerbils. Her thirteenth birthday had finally arrived! She had asked Mrs. Leeds for the day off work, which was met with wholehearted approval. She and Krissy had planned a day of fun which included brunch at her favourite pancake house, a movie and then the rest of the afternoon at the local riverfront beach, weather permitting. Laura had asked her mother if Todd could accompany them. Reluctant at first, her mother had softened when her daughter explained that Todd was struggling with a difficult home life and just needed someone to be nice to him for a change.

"He's really a good guy underneath," Laura insisted. "Trust me on this one."

"I trust you, honey," her mother said, hugging her suddenly. "You always tell the truth."

Except when I don't, Laura thought sadly as she hugged her mother back. *There is one secret I wish I didn't have to keep.*

The foursome had an excellent day. Laura and her mother were especially pleased to see Todd, normally shy and withdrawn in situations involving adults, blossom into a smiling, appreciative teenager who tucked into his plate of sausages and waffles like it was his last meal and laughed out loud during the comedy they chose to watch at the cineplex. He even withstood the good-natured teasing from the girls about his pasty "chicken legs" while they were at the beach. The dark clouds that had been threatening all day had parted as if on cue during the late afternoon.

"You really could use some sun, son," Laura giggled, tossing him the sunscreen. "Here, put some of this on or you're going to look like a lobster tomorrow."

Back at home, happy and tired, with sand in their shoes and their faces touched with colour, Laura opened her presents. Krissy's gift to her was a new plush cat bed. "For Maxi," she explained, nodding at the chubby feline sauntering across the kitchen floor in search of kibbles. Laura knew the present was actually intended for their fabulous feathered equine friend who was currently sleeping on a pile of old blankies.

Laura's normally frugal parents had outdone themselves as their only child stood eagerly on the threshold of teenage life. The new clothes and CDs were wonderful, but the showstopper was the coveted Breyer Pegasus.

"Oh Mom, it's fabulous!" Laura cried.

"It is nice," her mother agreed. "By the way, I haven't seen your porcelain Pegasus statue around for a while. I hope nothing's happened to it."

"I, uh, wrapped it up and put it away in the closet after Maxi knocked it over one day and nearly broke it." Once again Laura found herself telling a white lie, and this time blaming the poor cat.

"Well, this one can live safely on your shelf with the others."

The final gift from her parents gave Laura a bit of a start. It was a new backpack, a black and grey Nike sportbag with a large central compartment and lots of zippered side pockets.

"I noticed your old one is getting pretty ratty," her mother explained. "It smells awfully gamey, too. What have you been toting around in there?"

Laura, Krissy and Todd avoided looking at each other, because they knew they would burst out laughing if their eyes met.

Todd stood up and reached into his jeans pocket. He handed Laura an envelope. She opened it. There was a cheap dollar-store greeting card inside with kittens on it. The careful handwriting read:

Happy Birthday and thanks for everything.

Underneath, Todd had written, as an afterthought:

If you ever want to go fishing
I have a net I don't need anymore.

Laura and her friends presented the new bed and backpack to Flash, who was surprised and delighted they had thought of him. He circled a few times in the soft, fuzzy bed, then sank down gratefully in its plush comfort. "Ahhhh," he sighed.

He was equally enthralled with the new backpack, or Flashmobile, as the kids had dubbed it. "Very roomy," he observed. "The mesh is a nice touch, better air flow, you see."

As Maxi slunk into the closet and began to make herself at home in Flash's new bed, he yelled, "Hey! Get out of there!" and stormed in after her to defend his new sleeping quarters. There was the sound of a scuffle, the flutter of wings, a hiss.

Laura laughed. "Oh, they'll sort it out. They always do."

And so the Turtle Creek Triad began to plan the rest of their summer. Outside, the sky began to darken. In the distance, there was the ominous rumble of thunder.

A storm was coming.

SUSAN STAFFORD
"The Fearless Editor"

Susan Stafford was bitten by the horse bug at an early age, finally realizing her dream of horse ownership in her early twenties. She is the managing editor of *Horsepower Magazine* which helps horse-crazy kids satisfy their hunger for all things equine. Susan has three grown children and lives on the shores of Lake Erie with her husband. *Pocket Pegasus* is her first book.